To Oscar and Harry—my best boys!
—M.M.

To Laurie and James
—P.M.

E
MAH

Text copyright © 2000 by Margaret Mahy
Illustrations copyright © 2000 by Patricia MacCarthy

First American edition 2000 published by Orchard Books
Published simultaneously in Great Britain by Frances Lincoln Limited

Margaret Mahy and Patricia MacCarthy assert the moral right to be identified as the author and illustrator of this work.

Orchard Books
A Grolier Company
95 Madison Avenue
New York, NY 10016

Manufactured in China by Imago Publishing Ltd.
A Vanessa Hamilton Book
Book design by Mark Foster

The text of this book is set in 18/22 point Dante.
The illustrations are rendered in acrylic paints.

10 9 8 7 6 5 4 3 2 1

Library of Congress Cataloging-in-Publication Data

Mahy, Margaret.
    Down the dragon's tongue / by Margaret Mahy ; illustrated by Patricia MacCarthy.—
1st American ed.
        p.   cm.
    Summary: When twins Harry and Miranda bring their buttoned-down father to the playground, he discovers that he does not want to stop sliding down the dragon's-tongue slide.
    ISBN 0-531-30272-5 (alk. paper)
    [1. Playgrounds—Fiction. 2. Fathers—Fiction.] I. MacCarthy, Patricia, ill. II. Title.
PZ7.M2773 Dp 2000   [E]—dc21   99-50070

MARGARET MAHY

Illustrated by Patricia MacCarthy

Down the Dragon's Tongue

Orchard Books • New York

Mr. Prospero was a businessman with a big office and a computer. He was always neatly dressed in a white shirt, silver-rimmed glasses, and a beautiful, bright tie. Above his desk a sign said,

> # *You can do it!*
> # *You can do it!*

and Mr. Prospero always did manage to do it, whatever *it* happened to be, and to do it neatly too.

But things never seemed to be nearly as neat when Mr. Prospero went home.

"Daddy!" shouted his twins, Harry and Miranda, when he came home one evening. "Take us to the playground.

We want to go down the great big, slippery slide. Take us now! Please!"

"But I'm wearing a white shirt, polished shoes, and a hand-painted silk tie that looks like fruit salad," protested Mr. Prospero. "The playground is full of puddles and sand."

"No, no, no! Now! Now! Now!" begged the twins, dancing around their father.

"Woof!" barked Lollop, the family dog, dancing too.

"Yes, dear, please take them!" sang out his wife. Mrs. Prospero worked at home as a songwriter, and she was used to lots of noise and to things *not* being in their proper places. But now she was halfway through writing a song, and she longed for peace and quiet so that she could hear exactly how it sounded.

"We *must* go down that great big, slippery slide," said Harry. "We want to go

swizz!

We must go

swoosh!"

"We want to go *whizz!* We must go *whoosh!"*

sang Miranda.

"Daddy, you won't get dirty just *watching* us *whoosh*. We'll take good care of you."

"Oh, all right then," said Mr. Prospero. "Let's go." So down the road they went to the great big, slippery slide.

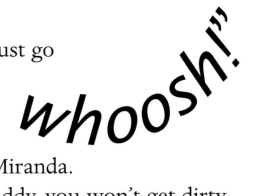

It was a lovely evening. The playground was like a bowl full of deep, golden light. The swings, the seesaw, and the merry-go-round glowed like treasures. But the great big, slippery slide running down the hillside was the loveliest treasure of all. It shone like the bright, long tongue of a friendly dragon.

"Once down the slide, and then we'll go home," said Mr. Prospero, stepping carefully over a puddle.

"But Daddy, now that you're here, *you* have to go down the slide too," cried Harry.

"Yes, Daddy! We're too scared to go down the slide by ourselves," said Miranda. "We need a father sliding with us. And a dog!"

"Dogs don't go on slides," said Mr. Prospero sternly. "And neither do fathers—at least, not fathers wearing white shirts, shiny shoes, and hand-painted silk ties that look like fruit salad."

"Please, Daddy, please!" begged Harry. "You won't get dirty. Look. The slide is as clean as a dragon's tongue."

Mr. Prospero looked up at the top of the slide. For someone who always managed to do it, whatever *it* was, Mr. Prospero was not so sure about doing *this*.

"Daddy!" said Harry, tugging at his father's sleeve. "Please!"

"We need a daddy to weigh us down," said Miranda, hugging her father, "just in case the dragon yawns while we're *whooshing* down its tongue."

"Well," said Mr. Prospero, "perhaps just this once."

So the three of them, followed by Lollop, climbed up, up, up, up—right to the top of the great big, slippery slide. Then they looked down.

"Aren't we *high!*"
exclaimed Miranda.
"We're at the very
tip-top of the top of
everything," cried Harry.
"Aren't we *brave!*"

"We certainly are," agreed Mr. Prospero, staring down the long, silver lick of the dragon's-tongue slide. The whole summer city spread out beyond like a land in a dream.

He settled himself on the slide with Harry on one leg and Miranda on the other. Lollop sat behind him, panting in his ear and tickling him with his whiskers.

"You can do it. You can do it," Mr. Prospero muttered to himself.

"Go!" shouted the twins. And off they sped, faster and faster, shooting down the dragon's tongue. Mr. Prospero's beautiful tie flew out behind him like a banner.

Whooosh! Swiiish!

Wheee!

Wooow!

Going at about a hundred miles an hour, they landed in the sand at the bottom of the slide.

"Are we down already?" asked Mr. Prospero with relief, picking himself up and brushing himself off.

"Again! Again!" shouted the twins, leaping up and down.

"Woof!" barked Lollop, leaping and licking.

Up, up, up, up, up to the top of the slide they went once more.

Whooosh! Swiiiish! Wheeee! Woooow!

The city glowed like a fairyland in the last rays of sunlight.

"But what's this in my mouth?" mumbled Mr. Prospero from the middle of the tangle at the bottom of the slide.

"Daddy's eating his tie," cried the twins, roaring with laughter. "He's eating his own fruit salad. Again! Again!"

And up, up, up, up, up they went to the top of the slide once more!

"Let's go down three times as fast this time," cried Harry.

"*Three* times as fast?" croaked Mr. Prospero. "I don't mind going a little faster—say, *twice* as fast—but *three* times as fast might be *too* fast!"

"Daddy, why are you looking so worried?" asked Miranda. "Why don't you laugh more?"

"Because of the force of gravity," said Mr. Prospero, smiling a little weakly. Then he settled himself and the dog and the twins snugly at the tip-top of the dragon's tongue.

Whoooosh! Swiiiish! Wheeee! Wooo

A strange thing happened. This time Mr. Prospero really *did* enjoy the great big, slippery slide. He laughed out loud in spite of the force of gravity.

"That was fun!" he said in surprise, picking himself up from under Miranda, Harry, and Lollop. "But what's happened to my buttons? Oh, well! It doesn't matter. Again! Again!"

ow!

"I'm tired, Daddy," said Miranda.

"And I'm hungry. Time to go home," said Harry.

"No!" cried Mr. Prospero firmly.

By now the twins were too tired to climb to the top of the slide, so they watched their father leap up the steps like a goat in a torn business suit.

They watched him slide down the dragon's tongue standing on his *right* leg.

"Again! Again! Up, up, up, up, up!"

Whoooosh! Swiiiish! Wheeee!

WOOOW!

Down he went once more, this time on his *left* leg, graceful as a dancer, his tie streaming behind him like a fruit salad that had learned to fly. The city was nearly dark now. Lighted windows glowed in the twilight. The twins cheered, and Lollop barked in amazement.

"Oh!" cried Mrs. Prospero as Mr. Prospero staggered into the living room. "What happened to you? Where are your buttons? Why is your tie dangling down behind you? And just look at your shoes! Harry! Miranda! I thought you were going to take good care of your father."

"He was too quick for us," said Harry.

"I've been sliding down the dragon's tongue," said Mr. Prospero dreamily.

Whoooosh!

wo

Swiiiish!
Wheeee!
Ooow!